THE MYSTERY AT Hollywood

Editor: Janice Baker
Assistant Editor: Sherri Smith Brown
Cover Design: John Hanson
Content Design: Randolyn Friedlander
Photo Credits: Shutterstock.com

Gallopade International is introducing SAT words that kids need to know in each
new book that we publish. The SAT words are bold in the story. Look for each
word in the special SAT glossary. Happy Learning!

Gallopade is proud to be a member and supporter of these educational organizations
and associations:

American Booksellers Association
American Library Association
International Reading Association
National Association for Gifted Children
The National School Supply and Equipment Association
The National Council for the Social Studies
Museum Store Association
Association of Partners for Public Lands
Association of Booksellers for Children
Association for the Study of African American Life and History
National Alliance of Black School Educators

This book is a complete work of fiction. All events are fictionalized, and although the names
of real people are used, their characterization in this book is fiction. All attractions, product
names, or other works mentioned in this book are trademarks of their respective owners and
the names and images used in this book are strictly for editorial purposes; no commercial
claims to their use is claimed by the author or publisher.

Once upon a time…

Hmm, kids keep asking me to write a mystery book. What shall I do?

Write one about spiders!

Papa said ...

Why don't you set the stories in real locations?

That's a great idea! And if I do that, I might as well choose real kids as characters in the stories! But which kids would I pick?

MIMI, PICK ME, PICK ME!

ME, TOO, MIMI, PICK ME, TOO!

Christina

Grant

Pick me!

6

You two really are characters, that's all I've got to say!

Yes you are! And, of course I choose you! But what should I write about?

National Parks!

Scary Places!

Famous Places!

FUN PLACES!

Disney World!

New York City!

Dracula's Castle

GRAND CANYON

On the *Mystery Girl* airplane ...

I CAN FLY US ANYWHERE!

Or aboard the *Mimi!*

Take me to the Forbidden City!

Or by surfboard, rickshaw, motorbike, camel ...

All great ideas! I can put a lot of history, **MYSTERY,** legend, lore, and **laughs** in the books! We can use other boys and girls in the books. It will be educational and fun!

Good stuff!

8

Where will you get the other kids, Mimi?

From my Fan Club! Kids can apply to be characters!

And can you put some cool stuff online? Like a Book Club and a Scavenger Hunt and a Map so we can track our adventures?

Of course!

And can cousins Avery and Ella and Evan and some of our friends be in the books?

Of course!

Can I apply?

And so, Mimi, Papa, Christina, and Grant took off aboard the *Mystery Girl* and America's National Mystery Book Series—where the adventure is real and so are the characters! —was born.

START YOUR ADVENTURE TODAY!

READ THE BOOK!

GO ONLINE!

TRACK YOUR ADVENTURES!

APPLY TO BE A CHARACTER!

1

HOT WINDS AND SHAKY GROUND!

Bump!

Bump! Bump!

"Yikes!" cried Grant from his seat in the *Mystery Girl*. "My lemonade's spilled everywhere!"

"Nice landing, Papa!" said Christina, handing her little brother some paper towels and chuckling. "Too bad I can't say the same for you, Grant!" She closed her book and placed it in her pink, flowery backpack.

"Guess what?" said Grant. "Papa landed right in the middle of a bunch of mountains!" He pressed his sticky hands against the window. "Wow, look at 'em!"

Papa grinned. He expertly taxied the little red and white plane down the runway of the Bob Hope Airport. "We're here!" he announced.

"Papa's an ace pilot," said his wife, Mimi, patting his hand. "And isn't it a beautiful day in sunny California?"

"Yep," Papa replied, winking at Mimi. "The Santa Ana winds have cleared out most of the smog—just for us, I think!"

"What are Santawins?" asked Grant, screwing up his face. "Did Santa win something?"

Papa laughed his big, booming laugh. "Usually winds blow from the west to the east, but Santa Ana winds blow the opposite way," he explained. "They're dry and warm winds. They blow out of the desert states, across Southern California, and out to the Pacific Ocean. They push all the fog and smog out to the ocean. That's one reason it's so clear today."

"Did you say smog?" asked Grant. "What's that?"

"Smog is the dirty-looking haze that hangs over a city," explained Papa. "It's a combination of smoke and fog. That's why it's called 'smog.'"

"Don't the Santa Ana winds cause fires sometimes?" asked Christina. "I remember learning that when we studied weather in science class."

"Yep," said Papa. "In the summer, they can be hot and dangerous. They can stir up fires in these mountains. And the fires spread like lightning because the winds are so strong."

"A lot of people say that when the Santa Ana winds blow, people act a little crazy. Anything can happen," said Mimi in a deep, mysterious tone.

Christina grinned at her lively grandmother who was always looking for a mystery. After all, Mimi was Carole Marsh, the famous writer of children's mystery stories. Papa flew their plane, the Mystery Girl, all over the world so Mimi could research her novels. Many times Christina and Grant traveled along with their grandparents.

"Do you think you'll find a mystery to write while we're here?" asked Christina.

"You never know," said Mimi, smoothing her short blond hair. Her blue eyes twinkled. "But right now, I just want to concentrate on the screenwriting workshop I'm going to."

"Papa, are you going to stay with us while Mimi learns how to write a movie?" asked Grant.

Papa turned his plane toward a small hangar at the airport. "No, I'm going to be right by her side," he replied. "I'll be fetching her coffee and snacks while she concentrates!"

Mimi winked at Papa. She slipped into one of her favorite red sweaters and buttoned it up.

"Grant, you and Christina are going to hang out with Brianna and Jeremy Reyes," she said. "Their mother, Elizabeth, is the manager of the Hollywood Roosevelt. That's where we're staying. They live right at the hotel and they'll show you around Hollywood. It should be very exciting because next week is the Academy Awards ceremony!"

"A Cat or Me Awards?" said Grant. "That's the weirdest thing I've ever heard!"

"Academy Awards," said Christina, slightly annoyed with her little brother. "They are a really big deal!"

"Academy Awards are awards presented to the best movies and actors of the year," said

Mimi. "The award is a gold statuette of a person they call 'Oscar'!"

"Oscar?" repeated Grant. He shrugged his shoulders and shook his head. "An award they call 'Oscar'! That's even weirder!"

"It's not weird here in Hollywood!" replied Mimi. "Anyway, everyone is preparing for all the celebrities to arrive. They are glitzing it up in Hollywood!" Mimi clapped her hands, making her rhinestone bangles jingle on her wrists.

"Mimi loves her movies," said Papa. He pushed back his black cowboy hat and unbuckled his seat belt.

"They'll be rolling out the red carpet for us, won't they Mimi?" cried Christina. She tossed her stick-straight, chestnut-brown hair and struck a movie star pose.

Christina loved movies as much as her grandma. The idea of visiting Hollywood excited her.

"Hurray for Hollywood," sang Mimi, closing up her red handbag and stepping out of the plane. "That screwy, ballyhooey Hollywood!" She threw her arms out wide.

Christina slung her backpack over her shoulder. She followed Mimi out of the plane. "Hooray for Hollywood!" she sang back. "Where you're terrific if you're even good!"

The two locked arms and danced down the *Mystery Girl's* steel stairway.

"We really need to learn all the words to that song," said Mimi. The wind whipped her short blond hair around her face.

Grant followed closely behind the duo. "Oh, man, I got my iPod all sticky!" he said, pouting. He turned on the music device and shoved it into his pocket. "I wish we could go to Disneyland while we're here." He plopped his blue ball cap onto his unruly blond hair and stuck ear buds into his ears.

Christina lifted up one ear bud. In a deep, low voice she said, "You never know what's going to happen. After all, the Santawins are blowing!"

Grant frowned at her as the group walked toward the airport terminal.

"They filmed scenes from *Indiana Jones* at this airport," announced Mimi, "as well as one of my favorite old movies—*Giant*. When I was a girl, I adored one of the actors in it. His name was—oh, my!"

RUMMMMMMMMBLE! Suddenly, the ground started to shake!

"Whoooooa!" yelled Grant. He yanked out his ear buds and grabbed hold of Christina. "What's going on?!"

"It's a little ol' earthquake," responded Papa. "Welcome to California!"

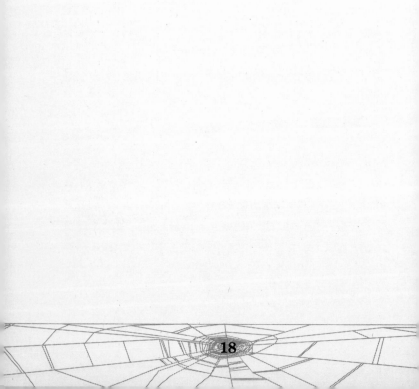

2
TAR STUCK!

"Don't worry, Grant. It was just a tremor," said Papa, driving their red rental car along the crowded California freeway. "Earthquakes happen all the time in California. The folks who live here probably didn't even notice it."

"Exactly what is an earthquake?" asked Grant.

"We studied earthquakes last year at school," said Christina. "My science teacher said an earthquake is what happens when the earth suddenly releases energy. The earth shifts and creates waves of energy that vibrate through the earth's crust. She said vibrations move out from the earthquake's center just like ripples do when you drop a pebble into water."

"Hey, I know what that looks like!" said Grant. "I throw stuff into puddles all the time."

"The closer you are to the center of the earthquake," added Christina, "the more you feel the vibration."

"I read that there are about half a million earthquakes in the world each year," said Papa. "Most of them can't even be felt, and only about 100 do any kind of damage."

"OK, kids," said Mimi, changing the subject. "Papa and I have a surprise for you. We're going to a special place called the 'La Brea Tar Pits'!"

"What did you say?" cried Grant. "Lab pits?"

"La Brea Tar Pits," said Papa slowly. "*Brea* in Spanish means 'tar.'"

"Yuck! Tar pits! We're going to pits filled with tar?" asked Grant, scrunching up his nose.

"Come on!" said Mimi as Papa stopped the car in the parking lot. "You'll be amazed. Let's go see some wooly mammoth fossils!"

A massive mastodon skeleton with long, saber-like tusks greeted Papa, Mimi, Christina, and Grant when they stepped inside the George C. Page Museum at the La Brea Tar Pits. Beside it, a giant, ground sloth skeleton reared up on its hind legs.

"Yikes!" yelled Grant. "I'm glad they're not alive!"

Papa chuckled. "So this is what Southern California was like before freeways and movie stars!" he said.

Mimi perched her rhinestone reading glasses on her nose. "This is very interesting," she said. "It says tar has been seeping up from the ground right here for tens of thousands of years. Water would cover it. When prehistoric animals came to drink the water, they got stuck in the tar and sank. The tar preserved their bones."

"Uggghhh!" shrieked Grant. "That's awful!"

"Those poor animals!" cried Christina. She gazed at the skeleton of a huge Columbian mammoth that had been found in the pits and reconstructed in the museum.

Just then, Grant backed into the fangs of a saber-toothed cat skeleton. "Yyeeeooow!" he yelled. He rubbed his bottom and gave the cat a disgusted look. Suddenly, a spacious, glass-enclosed room in the museum caught Grant's eye. "What are those people doing in that giant fishbowl?"

"It says here that they're cleaning and cataloguing the fossils found in the tar," said Papa, reading a sign.

Just then, a slender, red-haired girl in a white lab coat waved from inside the room. She walked out to greet them. "How do you like our museum?" she asked.

"It's cool!" replied Christina.

The girl laughed and said, "That's what I think too! I'm Kate Butler. I'm a paleontologist, which means I study animal and plant fossils. I grew up visiting these tar pits. Now, I work here excavating the site. We dig out new fossils every day. It's the best job in the world!"

"What's a fossil?" asked Grant.

"A fossil is the remains or impression of a prehistoric organism that has been preserved over the ages," said Kate. "Fossils are usually found in rocks. But here, the fossils are found in the tar pits that are just outside. This has been going on for centuries. In fact, birds, small animals, plants, and insects still get trapped in the tar pits."

"They're still getting stuck out there?" cried Grant, pointing outside.

"Unfortunately, yes," answered Kate.

"So all these animals lived right here during the Ice Age?" asked Christina.

"That's right," said Kate. "I saw you looking at Zed, our mammoth, over there. We also have giant ground sloths and saber-toothed cats."

"Grant met one of those cats already," said Papa, chuckling.

"We even have one human skull preserved," said Kate. "She's a prehistoric woman whose skull was crushed, and then she was thrown into the pit."

"How terrible!" exclaimed Mimi.

"Yes," agreed Kate. "People call it Los Angeles's first homicide! And then there are microfossils, like wood and plant remnants and insects. We have more than three million fossils."

"It's funny to think about prehistoric animals roaming around where all these skyscrapers stand now," said Papa.

"It is," said Kate. "Because of these tar pits, we know a lot about what went on right here in Los Angeles in prehistoric times."

"Ms. Butler, have you ever been in an earthquake?" asked Grant, wringing his hands.

"Oh sure, I hardly notice them anymore," she said, putting on her sunglasses. "I have to get out to the pits now. Be sure to go out and look at them. You will be amazed!"

The group finished their tour of the museum and took Kate Butler's advice.

"Whoa, it smells bad out here!" said Grant, wrinkling his nose.

"That's the smell of tar," said Mimi. "It still seeps from the ground out here. Be careful not to step in any. It's tough to get off."

"Look at the elephants stuck in the tar!" yelled Grant.

"Those are the mammoths," said Christina. She gazed at the life-sized models of prehistoric animals sitting in or near the tar pits. She thought about what it was like for the poor creatures stuck in the tar. On the other side of the pit, she noticed Kate Butler talking to another visitor. It would be fun to work here and piece together a mammoth skeleton! It would be like working a huge puzzle.

"Whooooaaaa!" Grant screamed suddenly.

Christina spun around to see Grant flat on his bottom, eyeing a tear in his pants.

"I'm sorry, Mimi," he said. "I think I got a little tar on my knees."

"That's all right," said Mimi. "We'll find something to wipe it off with. I'm sure this happens all the time." She and Papa hurried into the museum.

"Christina, guess what? I found something cool," Grant whispered to Christina. "I was picking it up when I slipped. I don't see any tar on it. It looks old." He handed her a small case with sparkling rhinestones on it.

"Wow, that's so pretty," Christina commented. As she opened it, a thin piece of parchment fell out. Written in purple ink were the words:

> Many years ago, I took a jewel buried beneath the Hollywood Sign. Please return it so I can rest in peace.

"What's it mean?" asked Grant.

"I don't know," said Christina. "But it sounds like someone needs help!"

3
WALKING THE RED CARPET

The red-coated doorman smiled broadly and opened the heavy glass doors of the Hollywood Roosevelt Hotel.

Christina gasped! A lush crimson carpet stretched the length of the Spanish-style lobby. A life-sized sculpture of silent screen star Charlie Chaplin lounged in a chair. Stylishly dressed guests sipped drinks from sparkling crystal glasses.

Christina spotted elegant arched windows and black iron chandeliers. A fountain bubbled in the center of the lobby. Tall potted palm trees dotted the room. A smiling woman in a long black gown played a baby grand piano in the corner.

"Now, this is Hollywood!" said Mimi, stepping onto the red carpet. "And there's my friend Elizabeth!"

Soon, Mimi, Papa, Christina, and Grant were busily chatting with Elizabeth Reyes and her two children.

"Brianna and Jeremy have read all your books, Mimi," said Elizabeth. "They're so happy to meet Christina and Grant!"

Brianna's brown eyes sparkled. "You've picked the most exciting time to visit Hollywood," she said. "The Academy Awards are next week!"

"Is that a famous movie star over by the piano?" asked Christina excitedly.

"We're not supposed to discuss our guests. But, yes, it is!" whispered Brianna, shaking her brown curls up and down.

"Brianna and Jeremy will show you to your rooms," said Elizabeth. "Then we'll meet for lunch and take a tour of the hotel."

"That sounds great," said Papa. He rocked back on his cowboy boots and gazed at the stenciled ceiling. "That's some fancy artwork up there! I'm looking forward to that tour."

On the ninth floor, Brianna unlocked the door to suite #928. Grant bounded into the room. "Awwwwesome!" he yelled. "Look, we each have our own chair. Our names are on the back!" He flipped around a black director's chair with GRANT embroidered in bold block letters.

Mimi examined the artwork and old photographs hanging on the walls. "That's a wonderful scent," she said, smelling a vase of multicolored flowers.

Christina peeked into the blue and white tiled bathroom. Four thick, white bathrobes hung on hooks. Mounds of white, fluffy towels and fragrant soaps covered the granite countertop.

Grant opened the small refrigerator. "Are these for us?" he cried, staring at stacks of drinks and tasty snacks. "Are they FREE?"

"They're all for you!" said Jeremy.

Grant flung his arms straight up in the air. "Touchdown!" he yelled. "Look at this gigantic flat screen TV!"

Papa strolled out to the balcony overlooking the pool. He stretched out his long frame onto a green chaise lounge.

"Grant, you and I could just stay here in the room," he said. "We would have the time of our lives!"

"Ooooh, look what I found," said Mimi. She lifted the lid off a box of candy and bit into a chocolate raspberry truffle.

Brianna and Jeremy beamed. They were happy that their new friends liked the room.

"Mama just texted me. She's reserved a table for lunch," said Jeremy.

"Let's go," said Papa. "I could eat a horse!"

At the hotel restaurant, Mimi studied the menu. "I want something with avocado," she said. "Artichokes and garlic would be good too!"

"Who does Artie choke?" asked Grant. He giggled at his own joke.

"Those are all vegetables that grow in California," said Mimi. "I think you should try a little of each, Grant."

"No, no, I can't eat a vegetable. I'd choke! Get it?" Grant grabbed his neck with his hands and made gagging sounds. Lemonade dribbled from his mouth.

Christina sighed and turned to Brianna. "How long have you lived here?" she asked.

"We moved into the hotel when Mom became manager," said Brianna. "But we've lived in Hollywood all our lives. Our great grandmother started working in this hotel when it was built in 1927. She was the head housekeeper. Our father is an architect. He worked on the restoration."

"That's interesting," said Papa. "I'd like to hear about that."

"He'll be here tonight," said Brianna.

"Have you been in an earthquake?" asked Grant nervously.

"Oh, sure, those happen all the time," replied Jeremy. "It's pretty scary when the ground shakes!"

Just then, Christina remembered the jeweled case in her pocket. She turned to Brianna and said, "Can you see the Hollywood Sign from here?"

Brianna laughed. "You can see the Hollywood Sign from just about anywhere around here," she replied.

"Can you get up close to it?" asked Christina.

"Pretty close," Brianna replied.

Christina felt a sudden urge to get to the sign as soon as possible. "Can you take us there tomorrow morning?" she asked.

"Sure, we'll take you anywhere you want to go!" said Brianna cheerfully. "We're your private guides to Hollywood!"

Christina fingered the jeweled case deep in her pocket. She shot Grant a serious look. Without speaking, Grant understood the mission. Poker-faced, he nodded yes.

4
TAP DANCING WITH GHOSTS

Elizabeth stood on the wide stairway in the hotel lobby. Papa, Mimi, and the kids huddled around her.

"Child actress Shirley Temple learned to tap dance on this stairway," said Elizabeth. "It was in the movie *Rebecca of Sunnybrook Farm*. Dancer Bill 'Bojangles' Robinson taught her how to tap up and down the stairs. That was in 1938. The hotel was about 10 years old."

Christina had watched all the Shirley Temple movies. "Wow! I remember that scene," she said. "They were dressed up like toy soldiers."

"Let's walk upstairs to the mezzanine," Elizabeth suggested, leading the way. "We have memorabilia from old Hollywood and lots of historic photographs. I'll show you one of Shirley in that scene."

"Look, Papa," said Mimi, taking him by the arm. "Here's the camera they used to film *Gone With the Wind.*"

"And here's a photo of Charlie Chaplin and Greta Garbo. They're at the hotel's grand opening," said Papa. "Brianna, I guess your great grandmother worked at the hotel back then."

"Yes, she did," said Brianna. "Daddy remembers Nana talking about all the old movie stars."

"There were lots of Hollywood events here in the early days," said Elizabeth. "Mary Pickford and Douglas Fairbanks were part owners of the hotel. They were very glamorous silent picture actors. They hosted a lot of parties."

"Silent picture actors?" said Grant. "You mean they couldn't talk?"

"Actually, the MOVIES couldn't talk!" said Papa, laughing.

"What?" asked Grant, scratching his head.

"The first movies were called silent films," said Elizabeth. "You just watched the moving pictures. There was no sound back then. You couldn't hear the actors talking."

"Whoa!" said Grant. "How did you know what was happening?"

"They wrote the dialogue at the bottom of the pictures," said Elizabeth. "You had to read the subtitles!"

"You would have to read really FAST!" said Grant. "I'm glad I don't have to watch silent movies."

"How big was the town of Hollywood back then?" asked Mimi.

"Not very big," said Elizabeth. "But the movie studios were all here. And the stars lived nearby and worked here. Now, everything is spread out. The celebrities aren't here much unless there's a premier or a special event, like the Academy Awards."

"I've heard of THAT!" Grant said. He gave a thumbs-up. "It's next week. Mimi and Christina think it's exciting!"

"It is," agreed Elizabeth. "Keep a look out for movie stars!"

Elizabeth swung open double doors leading into a spectacular banquet room with a glass ceiling. "This is the Blossom Room," she said. "This is where the first Motion Picture Academy Awards were presented back in 1929. It was a formal dinner event. But the ceremony only lasted about five minutes!"

"Wasn't *Wings* the first motion picture to win the Best Picture award?" asked Papa.

"It was," replied Elizabeth.

"It's about two fighter pilots in World War I who fall in love with the same woman," said Papa. "A classic old movie."

"Wow, Papa!" said Christina **flippantly**. "I didn't know you were such an old movie buff!"

"Well," said Papa, "it's about pilots! And you know how I love flying airplanes."

Grant squinted at the guests in the hotel lobby. "Does Mickey Mouse or Minnie ever stay here?" he asked.

"They never stay here," said Jeremy, "but you can usually see them at the Disney Soda Fountain. That's right down the street. But we have lots of other stars who stay here. Even some ghosts!"

Grant halted dead in his tracks. "D-d-did you say g-g-g-ghosts?" he stuttered.

"Tell them about the g-g-g-ghosts, Mama," said Jeremy, smiling at Grant.

"Well, actress Marilyn Monroe lived in the hotel for a couple of years," said Elizabeth. "It was when she first came to Hollywood. She was still a starlet, following her dreams to become a famous actress. She lived in a suite on the second floor of the cabana building. It overlooked the pool. Let me show you something."

Elizabeth led everyone over to the elevator doors. "See that tall mirror?" she said in a hushed and spooky voice. "It used to hang in her suite. Marilyn was very beautiful. She used to primp in front of it all the time. People claim they've seen her reflection in that mirror, fluffing her blond hair or putting on lipstick."

"Can you see her now?" asked Grant, peeking from behind Mimi.

"No, I've never seen her," said Elizabeth. "But I'd like to!"

"Me too," said Mimi. "I loved Marilyn Monroe in the movie *Gentlemen Prefer Blondes*." She fluffed up her own short, blond hair. "She sang a song called 'Diamonds are a Girl's Best Friend.' It became her trademark song."

"I think that could be your trademark song, too, dear," said Papa, winking.

"I've heard that song!" said Christina.

"I'll let you see the movie when you're a little older!" said Mimi. She flashed her diamond wedding band at Christina and smiled.

"Tell them about Monty Clift," said Jeremy, hopping up and down.

"Movie actor Montgomery Clift stayed in the hotel, too," said Elizabeth. "He liked to walk up and down the hallway, memorizing his movie lines."

"And he used to play his bugle out on the balcony!" said Jeremy.

"Yes," said Elizabeth. "And some people who work here say they've seen his ghost playing a bugle or pacing up and down. Others say they've felt a cold breeze brush past them when they've been near his old room."

"Like the cold breeze of a spirit?" asked Christina.

"So they've claimed," said Elizabeth. "Over the years, guests who have stayed in his old room say they've even felt him pat their shoulder."

"Whew! I'm staying off that floor," said Grant. "Which one is it?"

"The ninth floor!" said Jeremy. "Suite #928!"

Grant's mouth flew open. His hands cupped his face. "G-g-g-ghosts in my room!" he shrieked.

Everyone laughed.

But Christina did not laugh as heartily as she usually did at Grant's antics. *Ghosts. Something buried beneath the Hollywood Sign. And someone was calling out from the grave, asking her to find a jewel. Plus, she had to return it so that person could rest in peace!*

Christina hunched her shoulders and shivered. She felt as if a cold breeze had blown past her!

5
MAD HATTERS AND MINNIE MOUSE

"I hear you're interested in Hollywood's old architecture," said Miguel Reyes, shaking hands with Papa. Miguel had thick, dark hair and brown eyes. He was a taller, muscular version of his son Jeremy.

"Yes," replied Papa. "You've done brilliant work restoring this hotel!"

"Did you see any ghosts when you were storing the hotel?" asked Grant.

"*Re*storing the hotel," Mimi said. "*Restoring* means to return something to its original condition."

Miguel chuckled. "I didn't see any ghosts," he said. "But I'm sure we stirred up some! Hollywood was pretty run down until we started fixing things up."

"I want to stir up some ghosts! Stir up some ghosts!" chanted Grant. "I want to see one! Maybe Monty Clift on the ninth floor, playing his bugle!"

"Sure you do," said Christina, raising her eyebrows. Everyone laughed.

"Let's take a tour of Hollywood Boulevard," said Miguel. "You never know what you'll see there!"

"Look," said Brianna excitedly. "Here's Johnny Depp's star on the Hollywood Walk of Fame. It's right outside our hotel door!" She pointed to the name. It was etched on a bronze star in a slab of pink granite.

"Johnny Depp is the actor who plays Captain Jack Sparrow, Grant!" cried Christina. "And Edward Scissorhands!"

"And the Mad Hatter!" said Jeremy.

"And Willie Wonka!" shouted Brianna. They all giggled.

"Why are these people's names on the sidewalk?" asked Grant.

"It's a way to honor them," said Elizabeth Reyes. "Movies and celebrities made the town of Hollywood famous. The

Walk of Fame honors them. The names include actors, recording artists, directors, writers, and even people who worked behind the scenes. There are about 2,500 names along several streets, but mostly Hollywood Boulevard. More names are added each year."

"Here's Tom Cruise," Mimi said, staring at the star under her feet.

"Look, Snow White has a star," shouted Grant as they strolled down the sidewalk. "And Tinkerbell and Donald Duck!"

Grant was still looking at the ground when he ran head-on into a giant mouse— Minnie Mouse! She nodded her bulky head and stuck an ice cream coupon into his hand. "Look! Ten percent off an ice cream cone!" cried Grant, rubbing his head. "Minnie gave it to ME!"

"Here's one of Daddy's buildings," said Jeremy proudly. "It's the El Capitan Theatre. We see all the Disney movies here."

Grant couldn't take his eyes off the giant marquee above the El Capitan ticket office. Its intricate gold carvings sparkled in the sunlight. "If the inside is as beautiful as the ticket office," said Papa, "this should be something!"

Inside, the movie theater glowed like jewels of green, gold, purple, blue, and red. Layers of glittering satin curtains draped the stage. Carved, gold opera boxes jutted out from the walls. An elaborate balcony hung over their heads. Ushers wearing red uniforms with gold braids on their shoulders escorted moviegoers to their seats.

Grant plopped down on one of the red upholstered seats. "What is that weird music?" he asked.

Miguel Reyes laughed. "That weird music is the Mighty Wurlitzer pipe organ," he said. "It plays between performances. There hasn't been a theater this grand since the heyday of old Hollywood!"

"Mr. Reyes, what do you mean by heyday?" asked Christina.

"Hollywood's heyday is also called its Golden Age," said Miguel. "It began with the first talking movie, *The Jazz Singer*, in 1927. And it lasted until the late 1950s. The invention of television helped bring it to its end. But in general, things just declined. More and more movies were made away from Hollywood. In time, fewer stars lived and worked here."

"I would like to see a movie here sometime," said Christina as they walked back to the theater's lobby.

"It's really fun when a new Disney movie opens," said Brianna. "They have a live stage show with singers, dancers, and all the Disney characters."

"How about some ice cream?" asked Elizabeth. "The Disney Soda Fountain is next door."

"Yesssss!" said Grant. "I can use my coupon." He scrambled back out to the sidewalk. "Look! What's Spiderman doing on Hollywood Boulevard? Christina, take a picture of me and Spidey!"

"Like I said, you never know what you'll see in Hollywood!" said Miguel.

Grant and Jeremy posed next to Spiderman, bending their arms to show off their scrawny biceps muscles. SNAP! Christina giggled at the picture. She was shoving her camera back into her backpack when Brianna tapped her on the shoulder. "Christina, look up at that hill over there," she said, pointing.

It was the famous Hollywood sign—the word HOLLYWOOD on a hillside peeking between the buildings and traffic lights.

"Wow!" Christina said. "There it is!" Then she remembered. "Brianna, I need to show you something," she whispered. She reached back into her backpack. "It's a secret." She pulled out the jeweled case. Then, she unlatched it and opened the note.

Brianna's eyes grew wide.

"You and Jeremy have to take us up to the Hollywood Sign," Christina said.

"Whooa," said Brianna, gulping. She read the note again.

6
MUGGING WITH LUCY

"Wow, look at all these people," shouted Grant. "There must be a million of them!" The wind tossed his curly hair in all directions. "The Santawins sure are blowing today!"

It was mid-morning as the kids and Miguel Reyes stepped out onto the hustle and bustle of Hollywood Boulevard. Mimi and Papa had gone to Mimi's screenwriting workshop. Brianna and Jeremy were ready to show off their neighborhood.

"OK, kids," said Miguel, "I'm working right here in town today. If you need anything, text me." He waved goodbye as he walked away.

"Let's cross over the street and walk on the other side," said Brianna. "That way, we'll be heading in the direction of the Hollywood Sign."

Christina grabbed Grant's hand and waited for the light to change to green.

"Aaaahhh, what's this place?" Grant asked when they got to the other side.

"That's Madame Tussauds Wax Museum," said Jeremy. "It's cool."

Grant bumped into a wax figure on the sidewalk in front of the museum. "Whoops! I thought that was a real person," he said.

"They sure look real, don't they?" said Brianna. "We'll come back here later."

Grant bent forward to read the names of the stars on the sidewalk as he walked. "I don't know any of these people," he pouted.

"You know Shrek," said Christina, spotting Shrek's star on the sidewalk. "And look, here's Michael Jackson. And here's Mickey Mouse."

"I mean, I don't know MOST of these people," said Grant, still bent forward. BAM! He collided with a red-headed lady wearing a blue and white polka-dotted dress and a splash of ruby red lipstick.

"It's I Love Lucy," shouted Jeremy. "Take your picture with her."

Christina grabbed her camera, and Grant and Lucy grinned.

"Who was that?" asked Grant when the picture taking was over.

"You know, I Love Lucy. She's on those old black and white shows on TV," replied Jeremy.

"Her name is Lucille Ball. She was a very funny lady," explained Brianna. "She's dead now. That's just someone dressed up like her."

"Hmmm," said Grant, warily.

"I see Nicole Kidman's star," said Christina.

"And here's Matt Damon," said Brianna. "He's a real big movie star. He stayed at the hotel last year during the Academy Awards. He's really cute."

"You're so lucky," said Christina. "I want to see some movie stars."

"Well, look right over your shoulder then," Brianna whispered. "Because there's Taylor Swift!"

Christina spun around. One of her idols, Taylor Swift, was walking towards her!

Taylor's wavy blond hair blew in the soft breeze. Christina's knees locked. Her mouth flew open, but nothing came out. She was speechless. Taylor smiled, waved, and walked by the kids.

"She's so beautiful! And so tall!" Christina finally said. "I can't believe I really saw a star!"

"Happens every day," said Brianna, giggling.

Suddenly, Grant yanked on Christina's backpack. "Christina," he whispered. "I feel creepy. I think that red-headed Lucy lady is following us!"

Christina whirled around. The red-headed Lucy lady was staring intently at them. Christina stared back. Lucy quickly backed up and slipped around the corner. *What was that all about?* Christina wondered.

7
WATCH OUT FOR WET CEMENT!

"Don't worry about Lucy," said Jeremy as the group continued walking down the street. "She's out here all the time. She sells tickets to the Homes of the Stars Tour."

"I don't know," said Grant, looking uneasy. "Something about her spooks me."

"Hey, guys," said Brianna. "Let's stop here for a minute. This place gets really crowded in the afternoons."

The kids stood in front of a giant red Chinese pagoda with a copper roof. A huge dragon etched in stone snaked its way up the front of the building. Two stone lions guarded the main entrance. Three sets of carved copper doors led into the theater.

"Wow!" cried Christina. "This is where the movie stars put their handprints and footprints in cement, isn't it? I've always wanted to see this."

"Yes, this is Grauman's Chinese Theatre," said Brianna. "And this is the front courtyard area where all the footprints are."

"They put their hands and feet in the wet cement for just a minute," Brianna explained. "When the cement dries, their prints are there forever!"

"Oh, I get it," Grant said. "Sounds awesome. I love sticking my hands in gooey stuff!"

Brianna and Jeremy giggled. "They stick more than their hands and feet in the wet cement," said Brianna.

"Yeah, look here," said Jeremy. "R2D2 from *Star Wars* left his tread marks!"

"John Wayne left his fist mark," said Brianna. "It's right here."

"This guy put his nose in the cement," yelled Grant. "Here's another guy who put his mouth in the cement. Now that's kind of gross!"

Christina walked and gazed down at the handprints and footprints. She was entranced. The kids were right. A lot of celebrities had made imprints of other things along with their names and body parts. A cigar. A hair braid. Ice skate blades. A pair of wire-frame eyeglasses.

"Why do they do this?" she asked Brianna.

"Mama says they want to leave their trademark along with their prints," answered Brianna. "You know, something they're famous for. See, here are the kids who played in the *Harry Potter* movie. They left their wand prints."

Christina heard Grant whooping from the other side of the courtyard.

"Look! This Roy Rogers guy brought his horse with him," he yelled. "Here are his horse's footprints!"

"I think that's 'hoof' prints," said Christina. She giggled. Grant could be so funny without meaning to be. She looked down again. "Look, here's Marilyn Monroe," she said. "She wasn't a starlet when she did this."

"Yep," said Brianna. "She got pretty famous!"

Christina walked on. She knelt down next to some tiny handprints belonging to Shirley Temple. She placed her hands in Shirley's prints. *Just think*, she thought, *she was so little but so famous!*

All of a sudden, Grant shrieked. "Christina, help me!" he screamed.

Christina scrambled up, searching the growing throng of people for her little brother. "Grant, where are you?" she yelled.

She spotted him facedown in the corner of the courtyard, his **extremities** splayed out in all directions. His chin was sinking into wet, gray cement. Toppled orange cones and a KEEP OUT sign lay next to him.

Christina gently lifted Grant's chin out of the cement as Brianna and Jeremy came running up. "Quick, Brianna. Get a wipe out of my backpack."

"Hmmm," said Brianna. "Looks like they're getting ready for a celebrity signing today. That's why there's fresh cement here."

"It was that Lucy lady's fault," cried Grant. "I thought she was going to hug me, and I was trying to get away from her. Then I fell in the cement."

"It's OK, Grant," said Christina. She wiped the sticky cement off Grant's chin, nose, cheeks, and hair. "I wonder why she didn't stop. I don't see her anywhere."

Christina shivered. Something didn't seem right. *But why would Lucy be following Grant?*

8
CEMENT FACE!

"I think I've got cement in my nostrils," said Grant, wiggling his nose back and forth.

The kids were eating a snack at the Hollywood and Highlands Center right next door to the Chinese Theatre. From their bench in the center courtyard, they watched hundreds of tourists buying souvenirs and snapping photos.

Christina sprang from her seat. "Brianna, are those the Jonas Brothers?" she asked. She and Brianna stared intently at the three dark-haired young men crossing the courtyard.

"It might be," said Brianna. "Or it just might be three guys in sunglasses."

Christina wiped chocolate milkshake from her hands and mouth. Then she picked up her camera and started taking pictures of the stone elephants sitting on towering pedestals high above the courtyard.

"Guess what?" said Grant, watching her. "Those elephants remind me of the tar pits. Only without the curly tusks!"

"Grant, just think," said Christina. "You fell into the tar at the La Brea Tar Pits. Now, you've fallen into the cement at Grauman's Chinese Theatre? So far, you're batting a thousand."

"I'm leaving my mark in Hollywood!" chortled Grant. Everyone giggled.

"Smile, everybody!" said Christina. She clicked her camera. "Is this place all shops and restaurants?"

"Mostly," said Brianna. "But the Kodak Theatre is right over there," she said, pointing. "That's where the Academy Awards are held each year now. It's also where your grandma is taking her class. And there's a cinema and some nightclubs."

"You have a scratch on your chin," said Jeremy to Grant.

"Uh, oh," said Christina. "I just noticed dried cement on your jacket, too." She reached down to scratch it off Grant's sleeve.

"Great!" Grant said. "Mimi's not going to like that." He paused a moment. "You know, maybe I should have written my name!"

Christina spit out a mouthful of chocolate shake, and all four kids doubled over in spasms of giggles.

"G-R-A-N-T," Grant said, pointing his arm downward and writing in the air.

"You thought that guy was weird who left his nose print," cried Jeremy. "You left your face print!"

The kids howled with laughter.

"You could be on the news tonight," said Brianna, wiping tears from her eyes. "Tonight's headline: 'Grant leaves imprint of his face at Grauman's Chinese Theatre'!"

"Stop, stop!" said Christina, throwing up her hand like a traffic guard and trying not to laugh. "Let's get serious. We need to go to the Hollywood Sign. How do we get up there, Brianna?"

"Come with me, and I'll show you something," said Brianna.

The three kids followed Brianna as she led them up the stairs to the fourth floor bridge of the Hollywood and Highland Center. In the distance, they could see the letters H-O-L-L-Y-W-O-O-D sprawled across the hillside.

"Wow, that looks far," said Grant, picking cement from his eyelashes. "I didn't know it was on a mountain."

"It's not that bad," said Brianna. "More like a big hill. We'll take the bus part way and then hike. Jeremy and I've been up there lots of times."

"Let's get going," said Christina, slinging her backpack over her shoulder. "Time's a'wasting!"

"Look, there's Lucy!" said Grant, pointing to the courtyard below. "I'm not going down there!"

"Come on, Grant. She won't see us," said Christina, grabbing his arm. "I'll protect you, little brother!"

But Christina kept her eye on Lucy, who was chatting away and taking pictures with a group of tourists.

Grant has a habit of getting into trouble, she thought. *And accidents happen to him frequently. But he wouldn't have said Lucy was at the scene of his accident, if she wasn't. And if she was there, why didn't she stop to help?*

Odd, Christina thought, but decided she'd think about it later. Right now, she had to focus on a mystery and a climb to the Hollywood Sign.

The four hustled right past Lucy, who never even glanced their way.

9
WIND, FIRE, AND THE
LETTER "H"

Christina was starting to sweat. They were getting closer to the Hollywood Sign, but the road was getting steeper. She looked over her shoulder. Below them she saw rooftops and streets and heard the distant din of Hollywood traffic. The Los Angeles skyline spread across the far horizon. In front of them, the huge sign seemed like a **benevolent** protector, looking over all that was happening below.

Houses, jutting out of the mountainside, were starting to thin out now. The barren brown hill with the mammoth white letters loomed before them.

"Are we there yet?" moaned Grant from the back of the pack. "I'm tired and hot!"

"Me, too," agreed Brianna. "The Santa Ana winds are really hot today."

"Hot enough for a fire?" asked Grant, quickly checking the hillside for flames.

"No, that usually only happens in the summer," said Brianna.

"How about earthquakes?" asked Grant. "When do they happen?"

"Anytime!" said Jeremy.

"I wouldn't want to be up here in an earthquake," said Grant. "What if those letters fell down on top of you?"

"Actually, I wouldn't want to be up here in a fire!" said Jeremy.

"Let's stop a minute," said Christina, mopping her forehead with her sleeve. "How did this sign get up here?"

"They built it a long, long time ago," said Brianna, "before there was a Hollywood. It originally said Hollywood*land*. It was an advertisement for a neighborhood they were going to build. But then they started making movies here, and people started calling it Hollywood. Dad says someone took down the L-A-N-D."

"It looks bigger up here," said Grant, squinting up at the sign.

"Yeah, my dad says the letters are about 45 feet high," said Brianna. "That would be my dad stacked more than seven times high!"

"Tell them about the girl who jumped off it," said Jeremy.

"What!?" said Christina.

"Back in the 1930s, a Hollywood starlet jumped off the letter 'H,'" said Brianna. "She died. They say she haunts the road. People say they have seen her walking up here just like we are now."

"Whooaa! More ghosts!" shouted Grant in a ghoulish voice.

Christina looked over her shoulder. She saw a few Japanese tourists taking pictures. A lone hiker wearing a dark green ball cap stopped to drink from a water bottle.

"Why didn't I bring some water?" Christina said, stopping to catch her breath.

Brianna shoved her hand into her jeans pocket and pulled out a small bag. "Anyone want some California pistachios?" she asked. "They're even shelled already."

The kids held out their hands.

"I love these," said Christina, popping a couple into her mouth. "Of course, they're going to make me thirstier." She wiped her hands on her pants and pulled out her camera. "Let's take a picture," she said.

The kids lined up with the distant sign right above their heads. "That's good," said Christina, clicking the camera.

"What's that big white building over there?" asked Christina.

"That's Griffith Observatory," said Jeremy. "It's really cool. There's a huge telescope there, and you can look at all the stars."

"OK, let's keep going," said Christina. "Grant, you're going to have to climb under the fence."

"Why me?" whined Grant.

"Because I'm too big to get under it, and it's too tall to climb over," replied Christina.

"I always have to do the dirty work," said Grant, puffing up his chest with self-importance.

"We need to get to the back side of the letters so people won't notice us," said Christina.

"This way," said Brianna.

In another couple of minutes, the four kids reached the fence surrounding the sign. Now, they were right above the sign looking down.

"Grant, you're on," said Christina. She scouted the hillside to see if anyone was nearby. "Get going before someone comes. And stay low."

"Where am I going when I get down there?" asked Grant, crawling Army-style on his belly, under the fence.

Uh oh, thought Christina. *Where should he go?*

She stared at Brianna. "Look under the 'H,'" she said.

The kids watched as Grant half crawled, half rolled down the side of the hill. When he got to the 'H,' he began digging around with his hands. Christina strained to see what he was doing. The huge letter and brownish shrubbery blocked most of his body.

"I wish he'd hurry," said Brianna nervously.

"Come on, Grant, you can do it," said Christina under her breath. She noticed Jeremy's knuckles turning white from holding the fence so tight.

All of a sudden, Grant poked his head from behind the sign, waved, and started scrambling up the mountain.

"I got it!" he whispered, crawling back under the fence. Everyone huddled around on their haunches as Grant displayed a small, sea-green glass bottle. He carefully shook a tightly rolled parchment note from inside. The handwriting in purple ink said:

A star-bound rebel holds another clue.

"What's it mean by REE-BEL?" asked Grant.

"It's not REE-BEL," said Christina. "It's rebel. A rebel is a person who REE-BELS."

Christina looked up from the note. The ball-capped hiker, who had been following them, was just a few feet away. *Was it her imagination, or was the hiker staring at her from behind his dark sunglasses?* She slipped the bottle into her backpack. "Let's get out of here!" she exclaimed.

10
WRITERS AND
STRANGERS

"Hey, I can play hopscotch on these people's names," shouted Grant, hopping down Hollywood Boulevard. He stopped on a star. "Look, Bob Hope. I know him. We landed at Bob Hope Airport!"

"Quit playing!" said Christina. "We have to hurry. Mimi and Papa are waiting on us for lunch."

"Here's Musso and Frank Grill," said Brianna. "It's a pretty famous restaurant."

The kids scampered out of the California sun and into the dimly lit restaurant. Christina felt like she had entered another time. Red leather booths with high sides nestled into dark wood-paneled walls. Waiters in formal red jackets whirled around the room. *I feel like I'm in an old movie*, she thought.

Mimi and Papa sat at the front counter. "Come on in," said Papa. "We've saved four stools for you—and it wasn't easy!"

Grant immediately jumped onto a stool and began spinning like a top. "Wheeeee!" he cried.

"OK, Grant," said Papa, reaching over and catching his stool. "I don't think they want you to play on these. Your grandma only has an hour before she has to be back at her workshop."

"What did you do this morning?" asked Mimi, peering at her menu. "Hmmm, this chicken pot pie looks good."

Grant, Brianna, and Jeremy stared at Christina.

"We hiked to the Hollywood Sign," replied Christina. "It was a great view. I just wish I had remembered to take some water."

"Well, let's get these kids some water and some lemonade," said Papa. He motioned to the waiter who worked behind the counter.

"That looks like a pretty steep hike," said Mimi, looking closely at Christina.

"It's steep, but there's a road," Brianna said quickly. "Did you know they shot a scene from the movie *Ocean's 11* right over there?" She pointed to a corner booth behind them.

"Really!" said Mimi. She spun her stool around to look at the famous booth.

"Some of the stars stayed at the hotel while they were filming it," Brianna said. "We got to come down and watch."

"That's so lucky," said Christina. "I would love to watch them make a movie someday."

The waiter working behind the counter looked at Christina. "Little lady, did you know that this was the first restaurant in Hollywood?"

"No, sir, I didn't," replied Christina.

"In the old, old days, all the silent film movie people came here to eat. It's always been a hangout for screenwriters," the waiter said, nodding to Mimi. "The Writer's Guild, that organization for writers, is located right down the street. So writers have always come here; people like F. Scott Fitzgerald, William Faulkner, and Ernest Hemingway."

Christina was vaguely familiar with those names, but Mimi and Papa seemed very impressed.

"You'll know those names when you get older," said the waiter to Christina. "We also have a lot of famous celebrities who eat here. Some of them have a favorite table."

"Mimi, are you going to write a movie?" asked Grant from his perch at the other end of the counter.

"You never know what I'll do," said Mimi. She closed her menu and propped her red reading glasses on top of her head. "I like to keep it interesting! Let's eat!"

Everyone laughed. The waiter started taking their orders.

Just then, Christina glanced at the stranger sitting on the other side of Grant. *How can he see in here with those sunglasses on?* she thought. Then her stomach flip-flopped. The person looked just like the hiker who had followed them to the Hollywood Sign! The only difference was he wore a red ball cap instead of a dark green one!

"But why?" Christina said to herself. Her tummy flipped again.

11
A BOWL OF BEATLES AND CHERRIES!

Christina and Brianna sat on the wooden benches of the famous Hollywood Bowl. They watched Grant and Jeremy darting between the seat rows and jumping on and off the stage.

"I've seen lots of pictures of this place," said Christina, popping a yogurt-covered cherry into her mouth. She gazed at the bowl-shaped white shell that sat on the stage. "I just didn't know what it was."

"Yeah, it's a real Hollywood landmark," said Brianna. "They call it the world's largest natural amphitheater because of the way it's built into the foothills of the mountain."

Christina laughed. "Look, there's the Hollywood Sign," she said, pointing up.

"You're right! You can see it from everywhere around here!"

"It's really cool here at night when the Bowl is all lit up," said Brianna. "We've come here for a lot of concerts. There are fireworks sometimes. My grandma always talks about seeing the Beatles here when they made their first trip to America. They were the first rock and roll band to play at the Bowl."

"That's the one Paul McCartney was in," said Christina.

"Yeah, it was way before we were born," said Brianna.

"Can I have some of that water Papa got us?" Grant asked, running up.

"Sure," said Christina. "Papa made sure we have plenty of water and snacks."

"Gimme one of those yogurt balls," said Grant, reaching for her bag. "Hey, I know why they call this place the Hollywood Bowl."

"Why?" said Christina, taking the bait.

"Because you can fill it up with water!" said Grant, laughing hysterically.

"That doesn't make sense, Grant," said Christina, shaking her head.

"Well, then, you can fill it up with cherries!" he said. He bit into his yogurt cherry ball. This time Jeremy and Brianna joined in the giggling.

"Christina, it's funny!" Grant said, giggling some more.

"OK, it's funny," said Christina. She reached inside her backpack and retrieved the small glass bottle. "But we need to talk about our clue."

"Do you think it means a *Cafedrate* rebel?" asked Grant. "You know, one of those guys from the South in the Civil War."

"Con-fed-er-ate," corrected Christina. "Hmmm, I don't know. And what does it mean by star-bound? Is the rebel going to the stars?"

"Or is the rebel going to become a movie star?" asked Brianna.

"I just don't know," admitted Christina. She carefully put the bottle back into her backpack.

Brianna looked at her phone. "I just got a text from Dad," she said. "He's coming to pick us up. He's got a surprise for us. We need to meet him out front."

"Say cheese first," said Christina, pointing her camera at Brianna, Jeremy, and Grant.

"CHEEEEEEESSSSSSSE!" said the threesome.

"Nice one," said Christina. "I got the Hollywood Bowl right behind you. And you can just make out the Hollywood Sign in the distance!"

No one noticed the shadowy figure standing in the wings of the Hollywood Bowl, listening to every word they said.

12
FLYIN' HIGH!

"Awesome!" yelled Grant, giving a thumbs-up as he entered the flight chamber at iFly Hollywood. He wore a blue jumpsuit, goggles, and a helmet. Right behind him, an instructor closed the door of the glass, cylinder-shaped flight chamber.

Within seconds, a steady blast of air from the bottom of the wind tunnel slowly lifted Grant off his feet. The instructor held Grant's legs in a V-shape out behind him. He signaled Grant to extend his arms forward. Soon, Grant was flying about three feet off the ground!

Outside the glass flight chamber, everyone watched Grant, who looked like Superman soaring through the air.

"This was such a great surprise!" said Christina to Miguel Reyes. She unbuckled her helmet and shook out her tousled hair. "I never heard of indoor skydiving before!"

Miguel grinned. "Jeremy had his last birthday party here," he said. "He thought you would like it!"

"They use a flight chamber like this to make stars of action movies look like they're flying," said Brianna. "Once we saw some actors in here practicing for a movie."

"I bet Spiderman learned to fly in here," added Jeremy.

The stream of air became more forceful and lifted Grant a couple feet higher in the wind tunnel. Suddenly, Grant did a somersault in the air. He made a thumbs-up sign and everyone applauded.

"You might know that Grant would try some tricks his first time up," said Christina.

Grant started slowly spinning horizontally in the air. His eyes behind his goggles were as wide as the grin on his face. Even though she couldn't hear him, Christina could tell that her little brother was yelling with delight.

After everyone had their turn, Miguel had another entertainment suggestion.

"Why don't you kids go to Paramount Studios and take a tour?" he said. "I can drop you at the gates. You might even see a few movie stars!"

"Let's do that," said Christina to the kids. "We need to see some stars!" As they walked out the door, she said softly, "We need to see a rebel, too!"

13
SAY CHEESE, CAPTAIN JACK!

Christina gazed up at the arched gate that guarded the entrance to Paramount Studios. *I've seen this in pictures,* she thought. *Now, I'm actually going into a movie studio backlot.*

"Let's take a photo," she said, pulling out her camera. "Line up in front of the gate, everyone."

Suddenly, a Captain Jack Sparrow *Pirates of the Caribbean* look-a-like sprang out from behind them!

He motioned to Christina to hand him the camera. "Let me do the honors, mate," he said. Astounded, she handed the camera to him and lined up with the other kids.

"CHEEEEEESE," said Captain Jack.

"CHHHEEEESSSSSE!" said the group.

"Can I take a picture of you?" said Christina, gaining her composure.

Captain Jack stood between Grant and Jeremy and put his arms around their shoulders. "Arrrrrggghhh!" he said.

Christina snapped. Then, Captain Jack waved goodbye. "See you later, mates," he said, sashaying toward Paramount Studio's iron gates.

"That was so much fun!" said Christina.

Brianna and Jeremy giggled. Grant still looked wide-eyed. He jumped up and down as he followed the others through the gate. "Was that REALLY Captain Jack?" he asked.

Jeremy shrugged his shoulders. "I don't know," he said, "but he was cool!"

"Let's not take a tour," Brianna suggested. "Let's just walk around. Jeremy and I do it lots of times. This is the only big studio still located right in Hollywood. All the rest have moved away. These big buildings are soundstages. Crews are shooting movies or **episodes** of television shows inside them."

"Can we get in one of them?" asked Christina.

"We don't have a pass," said Brianna. "Let's go over to the New York City backlot. Something might be going on over there."

She led them to what looked like an actual New York City street with tall brick apartment buildings.

"Wow, this looks real," said Grant, licking apple fruit drink from his lips.

"Knock on the bricks," said Jeremy. "They're hollow!"

"No, Grant, don't knock on the bricks!" yelled Christina. She clutched her chest like she was going to have a heart attack. "We don't want anything to fall down on you!"

"Funny, funny," said Grant. "Hey, what's that?"

The kids saw a film crew, camera and lighting equipment, cranes, and a crowd of extras milling around.

"They're shooting a commercial with the *American Idol* contestants," said Brianna, pointing to a sign.

"Whoopee!" yelled Grant.

The kids rushed over to the ropes blocking off the filming area. Christina peered into the crowd to see if she recognized anyone. "Excuse me," said a voice behind them.

A young man in jeans and a yellow T-shirt brushed past them, waved, and ducked under the ropes. Christina and Brianna stared at each other. "Oh, my gosh!" said Christina. "That was Ryan Seacrest!" She giggled with delight.

Just then, someone yelled "ACTION!" through a bullhorn. A car careened around a corner and raced down the street toward the camera crew. It screeched to a stop. "CUT," yelled the bullhorn. "LET'S DO IT AGAIN!"

The kids watched the car repeat the same action. The bullhorn yelled, "CUT, ONE MORE TIME." After two more similar takes, Grant said, "How many times are they going to do that? I'm bored!"

"There's a lot of standing around when you watch a show being made!" said Brianna. "Let's find something else."

The kids sprinted toward a huge, blue sky with hazy white clouds painted on a wall. A sunken parking lot sat in front of it.

"What is it?" asked Grant.

"It's just called a blue sky. They fill that sunken lot with water to make it look like an ocean in movie scenes," said Brianna. "They shot the old movie *The Ten Commandments* here. They used the blue sky in the scene where Moses parts the Red Sea."

Next, they entered a park-like area surrounded by houses and buildings. "Grant will really like this place!" Jeremy teased.

"This section of Paramount once belonged to Lucy's studio," said Brianna. "They filmed a lot of other old TV shows here, too."

"Noooo, not Lucy!" yelled Grant, looking over his shoulder.

Just then, Captain Jack Sparrow sprang from around a corner. They jumped! "Having fun in Lucy Park, mates?" he called, cavorting past them and bowing.

Just then, Brianna got a text from her mother. "Mom says we're to meet everyone at Griffith Observatory to look at the stars," said Brianna. "Remember, we saw it from the Hollywood Sign this morning."

Grant dropped his empty drink carton into a bin. "So, we'll be surrounded by stars," he said. "Hey, just like the rebel!"

Christina turned and stared at Grant. She had been feeling unsettled about the mystery. Finding the next clue was like looking for a needle in a haystack. *Grant just might have something there*, she thought.

They began strolling out of Paramount Studios. Ahead, they could see Captain Jack doing a jig as he pranced down the street. Occasionally, he turned, doffed his hat, and made a wide, sweeping bow in their direction. Grant returned the bow. The two leaped and bowed until the kids turned out of the gate.

14

SURROUNDED BY STARS!

It was night by the time Christina, Grant, Mimi, Papa, and the Reyes family walked out of the Griffith Observatory. They stood on the balcony and gazed at the Los Angeles skyline glittering in the distance like tiny, sparkling stars strewn over a black canvas.

"That's a lot of bling out there!" said Mimi. The wind swirled her short, blond hair around her face.

"How high up are we?" asked Papa.

"We're on Mount Hollywood," said Miguel Reyes. "It's about 1,100 feet above sea level." He pointed to his right. "Hollywood is over there. And, of course, downtown Los Angeles is straight ahead. You can't see the other mountains since it's dark, but they're all around us."

"Did you kids enjoy looking through the telescope?" Elizabeth asked Grant and Christina.

"It was cool," said Grant. "There sure were a lot of stars."

"They were spectacular," said Elizabeth. "It's because of these Santa Ana winds."

"They film a lot of movies up here," said Brianna. "Did you ever see the movie, *Nancy Drew*?"

"That's one of my favorites!" said Christina.

"They shot one scene in the Griffith Park Tunnel," said Brianna. "It's the one where a truck almost runs over Nancy and her friend Corky. When they climb up a hillside to get away, you can see the observatory in the background."

"When I was a teenager, there was a young actor I adored. They shot a scene from one of his most famous movies here too," said Mimi.

"Who was that, Mimi?" asked Christina.

"His name was James Dean," Mimi replied. "He died at a very young age in a car crash. He was driving his new car too fast."

"There's a memorial to James Dean here at the Observatory," said Elizabeth. "It's right over here, Mimi."

"Oohhh, I wonder if his ghost is walking around!" shouted Grant.

"Grant, maybe we'll run smack dab into a ghost before we leave Hollywood!" said Christina, teasing her brother.

"I hope, I hope, I hope so!" chanted Grant, jumping up and down. They strolled over to where Mimi was looking at the bronze bust of her movie idol.

"Read this plaque, Christina," Mimi said, moving away from the memorial. "It will tell you about him."

Christina stepped up to read the plaque. "The name of the movie he made here was *Rebel Without a Cause*?" she asked.

"Yes," called Mimi from the other side of the balcony. "I'll let you see it when you're older!"

Christina pulled her sweater together. She shivered in the warm Santa Ana breezes.

Thoughts whirled through her head. *James Dean. Stars glowing in the nighttime sky surrounding his statue. The Hollywood Sign lighting up the distant hillside.*

"What's wrong?" asked Grant, staring at his sister's face.

"He's a rebel," she whispered.

Christina put her hand on the bust of James Dean. She ran her fingers around the edges of the monument. *It has to be here*, she thought. Between the base of the bust and the pedestal, her fingers brushed the sharp edges of a small piece of paper. With her fingernail, she flicked the paper out of the crack. It was a piece of parchment paper rolled into a narrow strip.

Christina carefully unfurled the paper. The kids peered over her shoulder, holding their breaths. Written in purple ink were the words:

> *The Sheik lives forever in Hollywood.*

Brianna gasped.

15
UP ON THE ROOF

The four kids scrambled up the stairs to the rooftop of the Hollywood Roosevelt Hotel.

"Wow!" said Grant. "You can see the street really well from up here. Look at all the people!"

"Marilyn Monroe used to live on the floor right below us," said Brianna. "She posed on the diving board down there for one of her most famous pictures. People say they've seen her ghost walking around the pool. Let's sit over there."

Brianna led them to a couple of white cabana chairs. They plopped down as Christina opened up her backpack.

"I don't get it," said Grant thoughtfully. "Shrek lives in the Kingdom of Far, Far Away—not Hollywood."

"Not Shrek," said Christina. "A sheik! The clue said a sheik lives forever in Hollywood."

"Well, what's a *sheik*?" Grant said.

"A *sheik* is an Arab leader," said Christina. "He's like a chief of a tribe or something. But I don't think that's what they mean here. Brianna, isn't there an old movie star called *The Sheik*?"

"That would be Rudolph Valentino," answered Brianna. "He was big in silent movies."

"Where is he buried?" asked Christina.

"Let me find it," said Brianna, looking at her smart phone. "He's buried in Hollywood Forever Cemetery. That's just down the street. It's right behind Paramount Studios."

"That's it! That's it!" cried Christina, snapping her fingers. "The sheik lives forever in Hollywood. Hollywood Forever Cemetery!"

"Well, that was too easy!" said Grant, snapping his fingers, too. "Good job, Christina!"

"We need to get there tonight," said Christina.

"Nooooo! Noooooooooo!" exclaimed Grant, jumping up off the lounge chair. "I don't like to go to cemeteries at night!"

"We'll be fine, Grant," said Christina. "We have to go. And we have to go tonight because Mimi wants to go sightseeing tomorrow morning. We're running out of time."

"I'm with you, Christina," said Brianna. "Jeremy, do you want to stay here?

"No, I'm going with you," said Jeremy.

"Oh, man," said Grant, zipping up his black jacket. "Let's get this over with."

enough," Mr. Cornwall explained.

Fran, nimbly leyof the lounge chair, "I
don't like to go to conclusions at night."

"We'll be fine, Gran," said Christina.
"We have to go... then we have to do things
because Mum wants to go somewhere
tomorrow morning... be tonight, put of time."

"I'll ask you, Christina," said Brianna.
"Jocasper won't past to stay here?"

"No, I'm going with you," said Jocasa.

"OK then," said Gran, getting up the
lounge chair. "Let's get this over with."

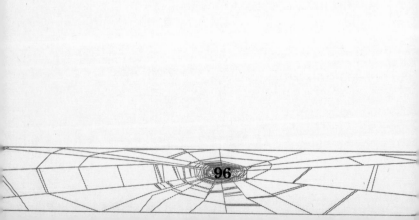

16
GHOSTS AND RED ROSES

"I'm starting to feel like the Hollywood Sign is following me around," said Christina. "It's like the moon."

In the distance, the glowing sign stared directly at them as they snuck into the main entrance of the Hollywood Forever Cemetery.

"I know," said Brianna. "It's even creeping me out, and I've always loved it. Look, here's a box of cemetery maps. Let's take one."

Hollywood's bright lights grew dimmer as the kids crept down the cemetery's dark roads. The rustling tree branches cast ghostly shadows all around them. The stench of decaying flowers filled their nostrils.

"It's spooky in here," said Grant.

"And its WAY too quiet," said Brianna. "I can barely hear the traffic noise."

"At least we have some moonlight," said Christina, looking at the map as she walked. "His crypt is all the way in the back."

"That figures," moaned Grant. He tripped over a tree root and bumped into a crumbling tombstone.

"These old statues are scary," said Jeremy, reaching for Brianna's hand.

"This is a really ooooold cemetery," said Brianna. "Rudolph Valentino died a long time ago. Daddy took me to see some silent movies at the El Capitan once, and I saw one starring Valentino. Daddy said his grandma used to swoon over Valentino. All the women did back then. There's a legend about how every year on the anniversary of the day he died, a lady dressed in black always visited his grave and left a rose."

"Does she still do it?" asked Christina.

"No, she stopped coming," said Brianna. "Everyone says she's dead now, too."

"Do we have to keep talking about ghosts and dead people?" asked Grant.

"I thought you wanted to see some ghosts," teased Jeremy.

"I've changed my mind," said Grant. "No ghouls for me!"

"I don't want to see any either," said Jeremy, stumbling into a rut.

"Here's the mausoleum," said Brianna.

"A maus-oh-what?" said Grant.

"It's a mausoleum," said Brianna. "It's a building with tombs in it."

"Oh, great," Grant remarked.

The kids crept up the mausoleum's white, marble steps and tiptoed through the arched entranceway.

Christina turned on her flashlight. Its beam shot down a long marble hallway. "I don't think anyone will see this light in here," she said, looking down at her map. "Follow me, it's all the way in the back."

Grant sighed and squared his shoulders.

The kids crept down the narrow center aisle of the mausoleum.

CRRREEEEEKK!

They stopped. Christina covered the flashlight.

"What was that?" whispered Grant, clutching her arm.

"SSSHHHHHH!" said Christina.

They waited in the pitch dark for several minutes. Finally, Christina flipped on the flashlight again and shone it on the map. CLICK. She turned it off.

"Let's walk further back before I turn on this light again," she whispered. "Keep your left hand on the wall. We need to get to the third hallway. It's the last one. Then, we turn left."

Skimming the left wall with her left hand, Christina led the way. As she walked, her hand fumbled over metal nameplates, flower urns, and slick marble.

"OK, here's the first hallway," she said, waving her hand into thin air.

"I can't see a thing," said Brianna.

Pointing her flashlight straight ahead, Christina swiftly clicked it on and off. "Follow me," she said. The four shuffled across the first hallway until Christina's left hand bumped into the next wall.

"The map says it's a short way to the next hallway," said Christina, moving forward and groping the wall. Suddenly, Christina felt nothingness again.

"OK, we're at the next hallway," she said. Christina looked behind her where the kids followed in the darkness. A wisp of moonlight filtered through the entrance of the mausoleum behind them. "Everyone OK back there?" she asked, facing the darkness where the kids stood.

"I'm fine," replied Brianna.

"Me, too," said Jeremy.

"I'm right behind you," said Grant.

Suddenly, Christina stopped. *Is that a shadow in the doorway behind us?* she thought. She held her breath. It seemed to pass by. "Let's get going," she whispered to the others in her bravest voice.

She quickly crossed the second hallway. *Now, another narrow wall,* she thought. She arrived at the third hallway. "We're turning left here," said Christina. "Keep your hands on the wall."

CLANG! Grant's hand hit a metal urn filled with plastic flowers. "How many dead people are we walking past?" he asked.

"Lots," whispered Brianna from behind. "Be careful!"

"OK," said Christina, "we're going to walk around a couple of sharp bends but when we get to the end, we'll be at the Valentino crypt." A few minutes later, Christina felt a wall in front of her. "This is it," she said. "I'm turning on the flashlight."

The kids found themselves at a dead end of shiny white marble walls and rows of crypts. Christina turned to her left and shone her light at the wall that bore the crypt of Rudolph Valentino. There it was—an ornate, bronze plaque with a glass urn on either side filled with red roses!

"Wow," whispered Brianna. "Wait until I tell Daddy about this. Actually, I guess I won't tell Daddy about this."

"Here, shine this on the plaque," said Christina, handing Grant the flashlight. She began running her hands around the plaque and the flower vases. Nothing.

"It's got to be here," she said. She separated the flowers in one of the urns. They were plastic. *I thought they were real,* she thought. She reached for the second urn of flowers and was rummaging through them when a rose stem floated to the ground. All three kids looked down as Grant bent to pick it up.

"There's a note in it," he whispered, handing it to Christina.

Christina slipped a rolled parchment note from the inner petals of the flower. Written in purple ink were the words:

> *If you want to be an actor, see Mr. Factor.*

"What's it mean?" asked Grant.

"It's a line from the 'Hurray for Hollywood' song that Mimi and I like to sing," said Christina. "Only I don't know who Mr. Factor is."

"I do," said Brianna. "He was the famous makeup artist, who started Max Factor Cosmetics. The Max Factor building is just down the street from the Roosevelt."

CRRRASSSSSHHHHH!

CLICK. Christina turned off her light.

"What was THAT?" Grant whispered loudly.

"I don't know, but we need to get out of here!" said Christina.

The kids left the same way they had come, stumbling and groping the slick walls and moving as quickly as possible. *At least this time we're moving toward light instead of darkness*, thought Christina.

When they got to the entrance, they stopped. Christina blinked. She felt a presence. There in the moonlight stood the dark, eerie figure of a woman dressed in a long, billowy black gown. The long black veil draped over her head floated in the warm Santa Ana winds. In her hands were fresh, red roses.

"Run!" said Christina, grabbing Grant's sweaty hand. "Run fast!"

17
WHERE'S THE RO-DEE-O?

The next morning, Christina lined up everyone in front of the Spanish-style steps and fountain. To her left was Rodeo Drive. It was probably the most famous three-mile stretch of shops in America. Palm trees swayed in the gentle breeze. Bright red and yellow flowers dotted the boulevard. Stylish people drove gleaming, sleek convertibles. Famous stores lined the sidewalks. Crowds of tourists gawked and window-shopped. Celebrities in dark glasses and floppy hats strolled the wide sidewalks.

"Would you like me to take a picture of all of you?" said a lady with long blond hair and sunglasses.

"Yes. Thank you so much," said Christina, handing her the camera and joining the group.

"One, two, three!" said the lady and snapped a picture. She handed Christina the camera and said, "Have a fabulous time on Rodeo Drive!"

"I thought we were going to a RO-DEE-O," said Grant, kicking the ground. "Instead, all we've seen is a bunch of old movie star houses and fancy shops. I don't see any horses or bulls. And except for Papa, I don't see any cowboys!"

"It's RO-DAY-O," said Mimi. "The name of the street is RO-DAY-O Drive. Why are you so grumpy this morning?" Her red high heels tap-tapped as she stepped onto a curving cobblestone street named *Via Rodeo*. "Let's go this way. We only have 30 more minutes before we have to meet our tour guide. I want to see this street."

"It looks like Disneyland," said Christina. She stared at the street's romantic archways and balconies.

Mimi peered into a window filled with chic clothing and jewelry. "It's fabulous!" she said. "I'm sure Papa could find SOMETHING for my birthday in this store!"

"Papa's signing an autograph over there," said Grant, skipping up to them. "Someone thinks he's John Wayne!"

Mimi laughed. "John Wayne died years ago," she said. "Papa would have to be John Wayne's ghost!"

Grant looked at Christina. His mouth gaped open. His eyes popped. He backed into a black iron lamppost and nearly toppled into a huge pot overflowing with purple and yellow pansies. Then, he ran lickety-split back up the street toward Jeremy.

"What's that all about?" asked Mimi.

"Who knows?" said Christina, shrugging her shoulders. "Wow! Look at that bracelet, Mimi. Your wrist would look good in that!"

Christina looked sideways at Brianna, who shoved her hands into her pockets and turned away.

"What's that!?" yelled Jeremy. He pointed to a sky-blue car parked at the curb. "That's a Lamborghini," Christina heard Papa say. "Isn't it amazing?"

"I wonder who it belongs to," said Christina. "Maybe some movie star!"

"I know we're walking by a lot of movie stars," said Brianna, "like that lady who took our picture. But who can tell with all the dark sunglasses and hats?" Brianna adjusted her own sunglasses on her nose. "I confess! I think one of the best things about living in Hollywood is mingling with the stars!"

"And I think one of the best things about Hollywood is all the glamour and bling!" said Mimi, eyeing another sparkly bracelet in a store window.

Glamour and bling! Christina thought about the rhinestone case in her backpack and the night they had spent in the cemetery. They had to get to the Max Factor building as soon as this tour was over and Mimi was back in her workshop.

She glanced over her shoulder. The blond lady was staring at her. At least, it seemed like she was. Who could tell with those big dark glasses? But something made her feel creepy. She clutched her backpack tighter and hurried after Mimi and Brianna.

18
REDHEADS AND BLONDES

"There's the Ripley's Believe It Or Not Museum," said Grant. "I've heard of that before. It's full of weird and creepy things. Don't you think that would be fun, Christina?"

"Grant, we don't have time for fun right now," replied Christina.

"Well, how about something to eat?" asked Grant. "There's Mel's Diner."

Christina tossed him a bag of chips. "We don't have time to eat, either," she said.

Plop! The bag of chips landed on the ground. Grant and Jeremy had disappeared.

"Grant!" yelled Christina. "I guess we're going to Ripley's," she said.

The two girls hurried through the museum's doors, but Grant and Jeremy were nowhere in sight. Instead, dozens of bizarre relics and objects surrounded them.

"Ooohh," said Brianna, gazing at the displays. "People used to make decorations from the hair of dead relatives and hang them over the mantle. Can you believe that? And the world's tallest man was almost nine feet tall! That's three feet taller than my dad!"

"Here's a picture of Marilyn Monroe made with more than 5,000 Czechoslovakian lead-cut rhinestones!" said Christina. "Why would anyone do that?"

Just then, Grant and Jeremy raced toward them, dodging other museum visitors. Grant looked panicked. "We're ready to leave!" he cried, bursting through the door.

"What's that all about?" said Christina as she and Brianna sped after them.

"Don't ask," said Grant, "but it has to do with a headless chicken and a two-headed calf!"

Right next door, Christina pushed open the tall doors of the Max Factor building, and the kids stepped through the dark marble archway. This was once the beauty salon of the stars. Now, it was the Hollywood Museum.

Christina thought the lobby looked like a huge gold, silver, and pastel-colored gem. Crystal chandeliers sparkled over gleaming white and rose marble floors, antique furniture, and potted palms. Christina's ears perked up when she heard the tune *Hurray for Hollywood* over the museum's speaker system.

"This is just what I think a movie star's salon should look like!" said Christina.

"Max Factor was the first famous makeup artist in Hollywood," said Brianna, reading a sign. "He liked to transform ordinary people into dazzling stars. He invented the first makeup used in motion pictures. He also invented lip gloss, pancake makeup, and false eyelashes!"

"Makeup for pancakes? said Grant. "Yeah, I guess my pancakes looked a little pale this morning!"

The two boys began giggling.

"No, it's not for pancakes," Brianna said. "It's thick makeup used to cover skin problems or even tattoos."

"Hmmmm," said Christina, walking slowly as she read her brochure. "It says here that Max Factor turned Marilyn Monroe into a blonde and Grant's favorite—Lucille Ball—into a redhead!"

"I guess that's what they mean by, 'If you want to be an actor, see Max Factor'!" said Brianna.

"Each of these four rooms is where he did makeup on celebrities," said Christina. "This room says, 'For Blondes Only.' This one is for redheads. This one is for brunettes. And this one is for brownettes."

"What's a brownette?" asked Jeremy.

"Maybe me," said Brianna, fluffing her hair and giggling.

"Let's work our way through these rooms," said Christina.

"What are we looking for?" asked Jeremy.

"I have no idea," said Christina. "Just keep your eyes open. Let's start here with the brownettes."

The kids entered a pale peach-colored room filled with makeup chairs, mirrors, dressing tables, and lights. Pictures of various brown-haired movie stars dotted the walls.

Grant plopped into an old makeup chair and started spinning it around.

A short lady wearing a badge that read "Mrs. Stone" instantly appeared. "Can I show you anything?" she asked Grant. "Have you seen *The Wizard of Oz*? We have the Good Witch Glenda's wig in the Hair Department. We also have a lovely red wig that Mr. Factor made for Lucille Ball. It's on display in the mint green room."

"No thanks," said Grant. "I'm not much into wigs."

"That's fine," said Mrs. Stone. "And we're not much into spinning chairs around here. Please jump down or I'll have to ask you to leave."

"I'm sorry, ma'am," said Grant, climbing out of the chair. He moved closer to Christina.

"It's OK," said Christina. "Stay with me. Grant, where did that guide say Lucy's wig is?"

"In the mint green room," said Grant.

"Let's go," said Christina.

The kids maneuvered around throngs of visitors to get to the mint green room. Once inside, Christina scanned it quickly. "Over here," she said to the others.

Christina stood in front of a wooden dressing table with a mirror surrounded by globe lights. The kids crowded around. A huge, color poster of actress Lucille Ball was perched on a nearby pedestal. A bright-red wig like the one Lucy wore in the poster sat on a mannequin's head on the dressing table. Framed pictures of Lucy, hairbrushes, makeup, hair clips, and tiny jewelry cases were scattered over the table.

"What a lot of stuff," said Brianna.

Christina looked around to make sure no one was watching them. She then started carefully lifting up items on the table and inspecting them.

"Look at this little music box," said Grant.

"Lift up the lid," whispered Christina. "But be careful."

Grant lifted the sparkly jeweled lid on the music box. Inside the velvet-lined case lay a tiny rolled parchment paper.

"Here it is!" said Grant, his eyes bright.

Christina lifted up the note and quickly opened it to the now familiar purple handwriting:

> Go to Madame Tussauds and find the Lady in White.

The kids scrambled through the crowd and out the door of the Max Factor building. Not one of them noticed the tall figure in a trench coat slip out from behind the poster of Lucille Ball. She flipped her long brown hair behind her shoulders and adjusted her sunglasses as she followed them out the door and onto Hollywood Boulevard.

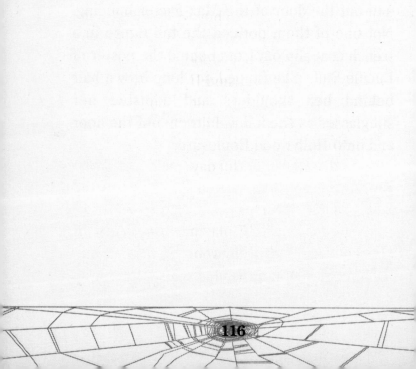

19
CAPTAIN JACK AND LUCY

Jeremy and Brianna led the way as the kids pushed through the crowds swarming Hollywood Boulevard. The gusty Santa Ana wind was hot. The sun beat down on their heads.

"You kids want to buy tickets to see the Homes of the Stars?" asked a Lucy look-alike, waving a brochure. She stood on the sidewalk outside the Hollywood and Highland Center.

"Not today, Lucy," said Christina.

Grant put his head down, staying close to Christina.

"Have a wonderful day," said Lucy. She waved goodbye and turned to an interested family of tourists.

Grant started playing his game of hopscotch on the Hollywood Walk of Fame. He jumped high and landed with a thump on

Kermit the Frog. Another thud, and another. "Look, there's Dr. Seuss!" he shouted.

"WHERE?" said Christina and Brianna in unison. They stopped dead in their tracks to look around.

"Here!" said Grant. He pointed at the star under his feet.

"Quit playing around, Grant!" said Christina.

"I've got to get rid of some energy, Christina!" Grant said. "It's tough doing all this sightseeing!"

"Look over there! That's SpongeBob Squarepants!" yelled Grant.

"Where?" yelled the other kids, looking down.

"Behind you!" said Grant.

The kids looked up as SpongeBob waved and giggled at them.

Just then, Grant spied Captain Jack Sparrow in the crowd. Grant waved and doffed an imaginary hat at Captain Jack. But the Captain looked away. He was posing for pictures with a group of tourists.

"He doesn't remember us," said Grant disappointed.

"He's just busy, Grant," said Brianna. "This place is a madhouse today. We're almost to Madame Tussauds."

The kids worked their way through the busy crowd of tourists gazing at the ground at Grauman's Chinese Theatre. Then, they stopped in front of the door of Madame Tussauds Hollywood Wax Museum.

Christina twirled around. She nearly plowed head-on into the girl in the trench coat, sunglasses, and long brown hair.

The girl slowly smiled. "Are ya'll going in here?" she asked.

"Yes, ma'am," replied Christina.

"Me too," she said.

Christina followed Brianna, Jeremy, and Grant through the doors of the wax museum. The girl entered behind them and disappeared.

20
PINK SATIN AND WHITE

At first, Christina thought she had stepped into a fabulous party by mistake. People dressed in sequined gowns and tuxedos filled the room. But then she noticed casually dressed people mingled with the elegant partygoers.

Flash bulbs popped. *Is this the paparazzi,* she wondered. Then, Christina realized that some of the people walked about, but others did not. It was as if some of them were frozen!

"Pretty awesome, huh?" said Brianna.

Oh, my gosh!" said Christina. "The people not moving are wax figures! They look so real!"

"This really freaks me out!" said Grant. "This is almost as spooky as seeing a ghost."

"OK, we need to find wax figure ladies wearing white," said Christina. "There are a lot of rooms here. Let's keep walking."

"There's the old movie star, Judy Garland," said Brianna. "She's wearing white. She was Dorothy in *The Wizard of Oz*."

Christina inspected Judy Garland in her sparkling gown. "I don't see anything," she said. "Isn't that a famous singer over there? I can't remember her name. Let's take a look at her." She headed toward the next white-clad figure.

"It looks like she's dancing," said Grant. He raised his arm over his head and pranced around the wax figure. Grant did one final spin and twirled into a woman wearing a Chinese-style red and black satin gown and elbow-length gloves. Strands of jewels hung around her neck. A red lace veil fell across her face.

"Whoa!" Grant yelped. The woman had grabbed him by the arm! She was not a wax figure. She was real!

Grant waved his arms wildly to free himself. The mysterious lady untangled Grant and smoothed out her skirt. "I am with Madame Tussauds," she said in a low voice.

"How can I lead you children around the museum today? Is there someone special you are seeking?"

"We're looking for a lady in white," Grant blurted out.

"We have many," she said. "Lady GaGa is in the next room. You'll find Marilyn Monroe signing autographs right over there. Keep your eyes open. There are many 'ladies in white' at Madame Tussauds." She nodded her head and glided away.

"CREEEEPY," said Grant, walking backwards to keep an eye on the veiled lady.

"Let's see if we can find Marilyn Monroe," said Christina. "All these real people and wax people are confusing me."

"Doesn't Marilyn Monroe's ghost haunt our hotel?" asked Grant, still walking backwards.

"Yes, remember that people say they've seen her in the mirror," said Jeremy. "I haven't, though."

"I know I don't want to," said Grant. "I'm not going to be looking in that—"

CRASH!

Suddenly, Grant was on his back with his legs up in the air. He had stumbled over a life-sized wax figure of actress Marilyn Monroe. She was sitting on her knees on a small, red platform. She was wearing a white sundress.

"Well, you found Marilyn," said Christina. She squatted down and looked straight into the laughing blue eyes of the Hollywood icon. "She's beautiful!"

"That's not all I found," said Grant, leaning over the movie star. He handed a tiny, pink satin drawstring bag to Christina. Christina gently loosened the drawstring and removed a folded parchment note with purple handwriting.

She had much fame.
This dotted her name.

"WHAT dotted her name?" whispered Christina to the others. Then, she opened the bag further. Something sparkled on the bottom—a glittery rhinestone!

"Christina, that lady is coming over here," said Grant frantically.

Christina looked up to see the veiled lady moving swiftly toward them. Her skirt billowed around her.

"Let's get out of here," said Christina.

"You children are causing a commotion. Madame Tussauds is unhappy!" the mysterious lady called to them.

But by then, they were out on the sunny, windy sidewalk of Hollywood Boulevard.

21
BURIED TREASURE

The kids stood in a row, leaning on the iron railing of the fourth floor bridge of the Hollywood and Highland Center. They stared at the Hollywood Sign on the distant hillside. In the shadows behind a pillar, a stranger watched and listened.

"I can't believe we hiked all the way up there," said Grant, slurping his orange slush drink.

"We've covered a lot of ground," said Brianna.

"That's for sure," said Jeremy. "And we still haven't figured out the mystery."

Christina opened the palm of her hand to reveal the gemstone. "We have the jewel," she said, staring at it. "But what are we supposed to do with it?"

"It's been like a scavenger hunt," said Grant.

"Yes, it has," said Christina, licking raspberry slush from her lips. "And out of all the places we've been and all the clues we've found, the really important clues are the first and the last ones."

She reached down, opened up her backpack, and dug out the first clue.

"Many years ago, I took a jewel buried beneath the Hollywood Sign," she read. "Please return it so I can rest in peace."

"We went to the Hollywood Sign," said Grant.

"And we found the clue about the rebel surrounded by stars," said Christina.

"We went to the Griffith Observatory and the James Dean memorial," said Christina. "And we found a clue about a sheik living forever in Hollywood."

"Then, we snuck into Rudolph Valentino's crypt," said Jeremy.

"We saw a ghost," said Grant, shivering.

"We saw a ghost," agreed Christina. "Then we found the clue about seeing Max

Factor if you want to be an actor. We went to the Max Factor building and found the clue about the lady in white at Madame Tussauds. We went there, and we found the jewel."

Christina looked at the rhinestone in her hand. "But I thought it was going to tell us where we should take the jewel," she said. "Instead it says that she had much fame. It dotted her name."

Brianna took a long drink of lime slush. "What does that mean?" she asked.

Christina thought harder. *The clue said the jewel was buried beneath the Hollywood Sign. It wasn't, but everywhere we go we see the Hollywood Sign.* She lowered her head. "We're at a dead end, you guys," she said softly.

"Is that a real diamond?" asked Grant.

Christina's head jerked up. She looked at the sign and back down at the glittery jewel in her hand. She snapped her fingers. "Grant, you're a genius!" she said. "Of course! I know where this belongs! 'Diamonds are a girl's best friend'!"

"Follow me!" Christina tossed her slush drink in a trash container and dashed down the stairs. Grant, Brianna, and Jeremy stumbled over each other in their rush to keep up with her. By the time they reached the last flight of steps, the ground was starting to tremble.

And the stranger from the shadows was close on their heels.

22
EARTHQUAKE!

The kids raced through the courtyard of the Hollywood and Highlands Center. People scrambled in all directions. Mothers yelled for their children. Vendor carts wobbled, spilling gifts and souvenirs. Plates and silverware rattled on outdoor café tables. Panicked waiters clutched trays of glasses.

"This is a pretty good one!" yelled Brianna to Christina.

Christina zoomed into the courtyard at Grauman's Chinese Theatre. The ground swayed under her feet.

"Look for Marilyn Monroe's handprints!" she yelled to the kids. "I saw them the other day, but I have no idea where. Grant, where are you?"

"Right here," said Grant, scurrying up beside her. "Is this a real earthquake, Christina?"

"It is! Everyone stay close," Christina said.

Christina grabbed Grant's hand, dragging him along as she searched the signatures in concrete. She saw Brianna and Jeremy a few feet away. People jostled her as they ran through the courtyard. Car horns and taxies honked frantically on the street. The shrill toot of a policeman's whistle added to the commotion. She glanced up once to see the Lucy look-a-like. Lucy had her arms around a mother and two children, who looked terrified of the trembling ground.

Christina's heart was pounding. She could hardly catch her breath. She bent forward, desperately examining the concrete.

"Here it is," screamed Christina. She raised her head to find the others in the chaos.

Just then, Mimi, Papa, and Elizabeth Reyes appeared in the courtyard. Their worried looks changed to bewilderment at what was taking place.

Christina dropped to her knees at Marilyn Monroe's signature in the concrete. Brianna, Grant, and Jeremy huddled spellbound around her. Christina leaned forward with the rhinestone in her hand.

Suddenly, a girl fell to the ground in front of Christina and the kids. It was the stranger who had been following them. She yanked off her sunglasses and long, brown wig. A cascade of red hair fell across her tear-stained eyes. "Please don't tell anyone she took it," she sobbed.

Christina looked up at her in amazement. It was Kate Butler, the archaeologist at the La Brea Tar Pits!

Christina took a deep breath. "Who took it from here?" she asked.

"My grandmother," said Kate. "I guess she pried it out of the cement years ago. I found the note in the rhinestone case after she died. I had no idea what it meant."

"I'm sorry, Ms. Butler," Christina said, patting her hand.

Kate Butler continued to cry. "She wasn't a thief," said Kate. "She was a good person. But it makes sense. She loved Marilyn Monroe. She'd seen all her movies. I remember her talking about how upset she was when Marilyn died."

"I'll bet she wasn't a thief," said Christina. "She just made a mistake."

"I'm sure at some point, Grandma realized she'd done wrong," said Kate. "She must have been too embarrassed or too scared to bring the rhinestone back herself. I didn't know what to do when I found the note. I just wanted to find the jewel and put it back for her so she could rest in peace."

Christina realized that the ground had stopped shaking. She reached over, took Kate's hand, and placed the rhinestone in her palm.

"Here, you're the one who needs to do this," she said.

Kate wiped her eyes with one hand. With the other, she gently dropped the rhinestone into the hole in the concrete above the "i" in Marilyn's name. A perfect fit!

23
DISGUISES AND KEEPSAKES

Kate Butler and Elizabeth Reyes came out of Grauman's Chinese Theater arm in arm. Kate still had tears in her eyes. Mr. Benton, the theater manager, followed closely behind them.

"This is a great day for the theater!" he said to Christina. "We had a minor earthquake with no damage. And Marilyn's mysteriously missing rhinestone has been returned safe and sound! Thank you so much for your sleuthing!"

Grant looked puzzled.

"I'll tell you later," whispered Mimi.

"I apologize," said Kate. "I'm terribly sorry if I scared you when I followed you around. I dropped the little case while I was walking on the grounds at the Tar Pits. I was pretty sure Grant found it. I panicked. I didn't want anyone to know my grandmother had stolen a jewel. But what I did was wrong."

"You were the hiker at the Hollywood Sign, weren't you?" asked Christina.

"Yes," said Kate.

"And Captain Jack Sparrow?" asked Christina.

"Yes," said Kate with a sigh.

"Wow, you were good at that!" said Jeremy.

"And the lady in black at Valentino's crypt?" asked Brianna.

Kate nodded.

"Whew," said Grant, wiping his brow. "That means it wasn't a ghost! AAAHHH! Were you Lucy too?"

"Yes," said Kate. "I was the Lucy who stumbled into you while trying to keep up. I'm sorry about the cement."

"How about the lady in the veil at Madame Tussauds?" asked Brianna.

"No, that was actually the lady who works there," said Kate.

"Whoooa!" said Grant. "I don't want to run into her again!"

"I'm sorry," said Kate. "Thank you for discovering the truth. I don't think I could have found the jewel on my own. And I don't think I could've discovered where it belonged."

"Here, I have some keepsakes for you," said Christina. She carefully pulled the jeweled case and the sea-green glass bottle from her backpack. Then, she found the folded up parchment notes and the pink satin drawstring bag. Christina handed everything to Kate.

After Kate Butler left, Christina and Mimi stood a few minutes at Marilyn Monroe's signature. Mimi reached down and laid her hands in Marilyn's prints. "Pretty good fit!" she said.

"She liked her bling, huh?" asked Christina.

"Yes, she did!" replied Mimi. "She was quite the glamorous star. She followed her dream to Hollywood and became a famous star."

Mimi put her arms around Christina's shoulders. "I'm proud of you for letting Kate put the rhinestone back where it belonged," she said. "I know how it **empowers** you to complete a mystery all by yourself."

"I do like to finish what I start!" said Christina. "It's kind of like following my dream!"

"I know what you mean," said Mimi.

"And I thought about you, Mimi," Christina said. "If you'd taken that rhinestone, I would've wanted to be the one who put it back where it belonged. I would've wanted to do that for you. Kate's grandma tried to right a wrong. That was good. And Kate wanted to grant her grandma's wish. That was good too."

Mimi gave Christina a hug and kissed her on the cheek.

"Yes," said Mimi. "And may she rest in peace now."

"Mimi, can we go to Mel's Diner and get something to eat!?" yelled Grant, running up. "I'm starving, and so is Papa!"

"And how about Disneyland?" asked Mimi. "Wouldn't it be fun to go to Disneyland after such a busy day?"

"Guess what!" yelled Grant. He skipped down Hollywood Boulevard toward Papa, Brianna, and Jeremy. "I saw a ghost.

The Santawins have blown me all over the place. I've been in an earthquake. And FINALLY, I'm going to Disneyland!"

Well, that was fun!

Wow, glad we solved that mystery!

Where shall we go next?

EVERYWHERE!

The End

Now...go to

www.carolemarshmysteries.com

and...

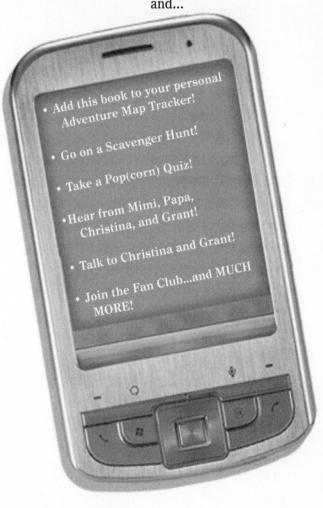

- Add this book to your personal Adventure Map Tracker!

- Go on a Scavenger Hunt!

- Take a Pop(corn) Quiz!

- Hear from Mimi, Papa, Christina, and Grant!

- Talk to Christina and Grant!

- Join the Fan Club...and MUCH MORE!

GLOSSARY

backlot: an outdoor area in a movie studio where large exterior sets are made and outside scenes are filmed

cabana: a hut or shelter at a beach or swimming pool

keepsake: something kept because of sentimental value

memorabilia: objects kept or collected because of their historical interest

microfossils: a fossil or fossil fragment that can be seen only with a microscope

ornate: made in an intricate shape or decorated with complex patterns

starlet: a young actress who wants to become a star

SAT GLOSSARY

benevolent: well meaning and kindly

episode: each of the separate installments into which a radio or television program is divided

empower: to make someone stronger and more confident

extremity: the hands or feet

flippant: not showing a serious or respectful attitude

Enjoy this exciting excerpt from:

THE MYSTERY AT

Devils Tower

1
CLOSE ENCOUNTER

Christina couldn't believe her eyes. The colorful disc hovered over the ground like a Frisbee. Strange, unworldly music poured from it and beckoned her closer. Christina spun on her heels, glancing in every direction. Her grandparents, Mimi and Papa, and her younger brother, Grant, were nowhere in sight.

I should run she thought. But Christina couldn't take her eyes off the beautiful disc.

The mysterious craft settled on the ground as lightly as a butterfly landing on a flower. Cotton candy pink, lime green, and aqua lights flashed and whirred around it like the gaudy rides Christina always rode at the Fayette County Fair back home in Georgia.

The lights danced faster and the eerie music grew louder. Christina watched in fear and fascination as the disc's side opened. Blinding white light poured from its belly and a spindly creature, not much taller than Grant, ambled forward.

Christina knew it was past time to run, but her legs wouldn't move. It was like she was jogging in a bowl of her favorite chocolate pudding. The creature crept closer. Christina's heart pounded. Bony fingers touched her arm. Christina screamed.

"*Whoa* there!" a deep voiced warned.

Christina's eyes popped open. She saw Papa's familiar cowboy hat above the seat in front of her. Beside him, her mystery-writing grandmother, Mimi, was typing away on her shiny silver laptop. The steady hum of Papa's little red and white plane, the *Mystery Girl*, had replaced the strange music from her dream. Everything was as it should be. Once again they were on their way to Devils Tower, Wyoming. Christina rubbed her blue eyes and stretched, thankful that she was no longer face to face with an extraterrestrial!

"That must have been some dream, Christina," Mimi said without looking up from her work.

"More like a nightmare!" Christina answered, still trying to clear the haunting images from her foggy brain.

"Well, maybe I shouldn't have let you watch that movie," Mimi said. "You always seem to have bad dreams after you watch strange movies."

The day before they departed for their adventure in Wyoming, Mimi rented a famous movie about Devils Tower—*Close Encounters of the Third Kind*. It was about a man drawn there to meet a UFO filled with friendly aliens. Christina had explained to her brother that UFO stands for Unidentified Flying Object.

Christina and Grant had traveled the world with Mimi and Papa while Mimi researched her mystery books. There weren't a lot of kids their age who had seen as many interesting places and met as many fascinating people as the two of them. And wherever they went, they had the uncanny ability to wind up smack dab in the middle of a mind-bending mystery. But they had never, ever, met any aliens!

Christina reassured her grandmother that renting the movie was a good idea. "You know I always like learning about the places we visit," she said. "I liked the scenes at Devils Tower. Now I know what to expect when we get there."

"That won't be much longer now," Papa assured them.

"Good!" Mimi said. She yanked off her red sparkly reading glasses and snapped her laptop shut. "The sun is getting low and you know I don't like to fly at night."

"I love to fly at night," Papa said. "That's the best time to see the pretty lights of the UFOs." He flashed Christina a mischievous smile.

"Oh, Papa," Christina said. "You know I don't really believe in all that UFO and alien stuff."

"*R-e-a-lly*?" a strange voice asked from the seat beside her. Christina watched the long, bony fingers from her dream peel back a blanket that she thought covered her sleeping brother. A shiny green head with bulging black eyes glared at her.

Christina screamed. Was she dreaming again?

"Grant!" Mimi scolded. "I told you not to use that get-up to scare your sister!"

"I should have known!" Christina yelled. She crossed her arms over her chest in relief. "Where did you get that?"

"Mimi bought it for me after we watched that UFO movie," he said. "Isn't it great? I'm gonna freak some people out at Devils Tower!"

"I think you'll freak them out worse if you take off the rubber head and show your real face!" Christina teased her brother.

"OK, you two!" Papa said. "If you want to get a good sunset view of Devils Tower, look out your window at 4 o'clock."

"But it's already past 4 o'clock," Grant complained.

"He means 4 o'clock the location, not 4 o'clock the time. That's what pilots say when they're talking about a position in the sky," Christina explained, pointing to the spot where the 4 would be on the face of a clock.

On the horizon, the Tower glowed an unearthly red in the sunset. It was beautiful, but bizarre.

"I thought it was gigantic," Grant said, disappointed. "I've seen anthills bigger than that!"

"We're still several miles away," Mimi said. "When we get closer, I promise you won't be disappointed."

"Uh oh," Papa said.

"What is it?" Mimi asked.

"We've got company," Papa answered. He turned in his seat for a better look.

Christina swiveled to see red, green, and white flashing lights gaining on the *Mystery Girl*. She pinched her arm, just to be sure this time. It hurt. This was definitely no dream!

2
UFO!

Christina watched Mimi's and Papa's concerned expressions and wondered if she should start believing in UFOs.

"The aliens are gaining on us, Papa!" Grant cautioned.

Suddenly a booming voice jarred their ears. CHANGE YOUR COURSE IMMEDIATELY! YOU HAVE ENTERED A NO-FLY ZONE! CHANGE COURSE!

"Wow!" Grant exclaimed. "The aliens speak English!"

"I don't think those are aliens," Mimi said. She flipped on a reading light and studied Papa's map.

"If they're not aliens, then who are they?" Grant asked. "And why are they telling us there aren't any flies here?"

Mimi tapped their location on the map and explained. "No planes are allowed to fly near Devils Tower," she said. "That's why it's called a 'no-fly' zone. Those are probably park rangers on our tail."

"Oops!" Papa said. "Guess I was so excited about looking at Devils Tower, I wasn't being a good navigator."

"It was an easy mistake, Papa," Grant said. "I read that Wyoming and Montana are often called 'Big Sky Country,' so there's plenty of sky to get lost in."

Christina nodded to help ease Papa's feelings. "Besides, we weren't close enough to smack into Devils Tower," she said. "I guess that's why they don't want planes flying anywhere near it."

"That's only one reason it's a no-fly zone," Mimi said. "President Theodore Roosevelt named Devils Tower our nation's first national monument in 1906. But for centuries it has been a sacred site to more than 20 different Native American tribes. Flying near it is considered disrespectful."